Poems

Freely Espousing (1969)
The Crystal Lithium (1972)
Hymn to Life (1974)
The Morning of the Poem (1980)

Novels

Alfred and Guinevere (1958)
A Nest of Ninnies (with John Ashbery, 1976)
What's for Dinner? (1978)

Prose and Poems

The Home Book (edited by Trevor Winkfield, 1977)

A
FEW
DAYS

A
FEW
DAYS

POEMS BY

James
Schuyler

Random House
New York

Portions of this work first appeared in the
following publications: *Mag City, Mothers of Mud,
The New Yorker, The Paris Review, Poetry
Project Newsletter,* and *The Yale Review.*
"The Snowdrop" first appeared in
The Temple of Flora, published by
The Arion Press, in 1984.

Library of Congress Cataloging in Publication Data
Schuyler, James.
A few days.

I. Title.
PS3569.C56F48   1985   811'.54   85-2018
ISBN 0-394-54685-7
ISBN 0-394-74126-9 (pbk.)

Manufactured in the United States of America
Typography and binding design by Jo Anne Metsch
9 8 7 6 5 4 3 2
First Edition

for Tom Carey

Contents

A
FEW
DAYS

The Snowdrop

The sheath pierces the turf
and the flower unfurls: drooping,
pendent, white, three-petalled,
the corolla with a frill
of green: the virgin of the spring!
In earliest spring! (Reginald
Farrer hated snowdrops: in his
Yorkshire rock garden the rain
beat them down into the mud
and they got all dirty. Why not
pick a few, wash them off and
make a nosegay in a wineglass,
Reginald?) And when the flower
fades and dies, the stem
measures its length along the sod,
the seed pod swelling like
a pale green testicle.

The Rose of Marion

for Harold Talbott

is pink and many-petalled:
it rests on the rim
of a shot glass on the desk
in my room in this
eighteenth-century house in,
of course, Marion, Cape Cod,
Massachusetts (for
further details, see Thoreau
or *The Outermost House* by
whats-his-face).

The window is filled
with leaves! So different
from my urban view
in stony-hearted New York.
I love leaves, so green,
so still, then
all ashimmer. Would
I like to live here? I
don't know: it's
far from friends
(for me) and others
I depend on. But
it's awfully nice to visit,
a whaling port
like Sag Harbor, Long Island.

Pink rose of Marion, I
wish I knew your name.
Perhaps one day I will.

Gray Day

"There is a cloud,"
Fairfield used to say,
"that stretches from
Richmond to Bangor:
its center is Southampton."
Today,
gray day,
its center is
Bridgehampton,
a nimbus over the pond
you made,
where a willow
jerks its leaves
and the oxeye daisies
stand in unserried ranks.
Helena is on a bench
by the pond, writing
a poem, I bet.
I opt
for the living room and
the squishy chairs
and Rachmaninoff
played by Richter
(who else?) and
here comes Oriane
with her ragged ruff:
"Oriane, there are hairs
all over my blazer:
would you care
to discuss it?" She
would not and stalks
haughtily out of the room,
leaving me with the music
and a window
full of leaves.

This Notebook

is small and stamped,
MADE IN ITALY.
It's bound in
Florentine art paper:
a design in blue and brown
of Maltese crosses
and what looks like
bladder wrack. How it takes
me back! To our
pensione on Piazza Frescobaldi,
Ponte Santa Trinità
(replaced, in postwar '40s,
by a Bailey bridge),
the Via Tornabuoni, and
Doney's and Leland's, in
one of which
Ronald Firbank
dangled grapes—before
my time. When
I walked in Florence I
used to see it not
as the Medici's stamping ground,
but through the eyes
of one of Henry James's
heroes or heroines:
Isabel Archer, perhaps.
To walk up to
Bellosguardo, to look
and wonder and remember
what I never knew!
Little notebook, I
love you, and the friend
who gave me you.

Lilacs

for Helena Hughes

Helena brought me
hang their heads
heavy with fragrance
—what other
is like it? roses?
lilies of the valley?
freesias? (not tube-
roses: they're
too much)—and
prove that fat
can be beautiful:
not on me, on them.
Each truss of seemingly
myriad, four-petalled
flowerets of that color
(lilac) Persia dreamed up:
would they could last
forever, were of porcelain
or silk: silk lilacs?
I
think not. I love them as
they are, seeming so
permanent, yet even
more transient than we!
Now I think I'll have
a sniff of lilac,
then eat a wedge
of rhubarb pie:
rhubarb and lilacs:
could life hold more?
Perhaps:
there is, for instance,
Helena.

Thursday

A summer dawn breaks over the city.
Breaks? No, it's more as though the night
—the "dark," we call it—drained
away into the sewers and left transpicuity.
You can see: buildings, dogs, people,
cement, etc. The summer city, where,
I suppose, someone is happy. Someone.

The other bright evening cabbing
down Fifth Avenue past the park I
saw all the leaves on all the trees
and counted them: not one by one, in
bunches. I forget precisely how many
there were: quite a few. Oh yes, more
than you could count. Not me, though.
I counted them, bunch by bunch.

As I said above, it's summer: not
my favorite season. I prefer the spring,
when the leaves bud and unfurl, or
autumn, when the leaves
color and fall. Or winter, when
the leaf-bearers stand naked,
flexing their biceps like bodybuilders
exhibiting their charms.

Then there is a fifth season,
called—but that's my secret.
Yes, my secret, and I'm going
to keep it that way. Yes, my secret.

Cornflowers

After the stormy night:
the crack of lightning and
the thunder peals (one bolt
fell in my street!)
the cornflowers (or are they
bachelor's buttons?) stand,
ragged scraps of sky, in
a shrimp-cocktail glass on
thin green stems with thin
green leaves, so blue, so blue
azure as sky-blue eyes
the cornflowers (I wish
I were wading through a
field where they bloom)
tattered tales of my life.

Velvet Roses

Katie is making
velvet roses: next
to a green pair, she
fastens a bunch of
wooden spoons. How
striking they will
look, on the bodice
of her dance frock!

And Anne is cooking,
and Lizzie is there . . .

Sleeping again,
dreaming again.

August First, 1974

was yesterday. I went out in the yard
in back today. I didn't stay: too hot
for comfort even under the apple trees
hung—smothered, in fact—by Concord
grape vines, unpruned, run rampant. But
then, my stepfather, the gardener, is
dead. The garden that he took such pride
in isn't much really anymore. I don't
mind it this way. It's dry (rain predicted)
and from this desk it used to be—say,
more than thirty years ago—you could look
right down the valley that leads to Olean.
Now, in August, the leaves of young trees
across the street hide all that view of
uncultivated fields, where sometimes
a horse would unexpectedly appear: Jim
Westland's. Jim's dead too, and Katharine,
his wife. So kind to me when I was
in my teens. A hot breath of wind stirs
a white voile curtain: or are they
organdy or net? It couldn't matter less.
Below the window a taxus hedge: Japanese
yew, so popular for foundation plantings
in suburbs and small towns. *Qualunque:*
commonplace. I like a house to rise up
naked from the ground it stands on. Oh,
honestly, I don't much care one way or the
other. And what's that small purple
flowered weed or wildflower that grows
in grass, making something like a herb
lawn? Typing this makes me sweat. No
more today. You see, I'm waiting.

Sleep-Gummed Eyes

for Geoff Young

With sleep-crowned eyes I
see the morning sunlight
lie, a pinky-yellow rose
petal, on the building
across the street: the radio
plays and says the day
is cloudy, overcast! How
can it be so different
between Twenty-third Street
and wherever in the Fifties
the broadcast originates? On
the building across the
street there is a stone or
concrete escutcheon: an
oeuf à la Russe or an *oeuf
en gelée*, a white egg in
pinky-topaz jelly. A funny
conceit for a downtown
loft building. I rub my
eyes and roll the gunk
between my finger-ends: it's
February first, 1982,
and they say (on the radio)
torrents of rain will
descend and the temperature
drop to well below
freezing. So be it.

Overcast, Hot

for Alice Notley

It's a hot day:
not so hot
as the days before:
it's *that* July,
the one in 1981,
the hot one. Alice
said, "I lay in bed
all night with
my face sweating."
I lay in bed
all night with
my ass sweating.
Darling Helena sends
a card from England
where it's overcast
and cool. Lucky
England! And
Prince Charles is
about to marry
Lady Di! "Will you
get up at four-thirty to
watch the wedding
on the tube?" Elinor
asks. Not
bloody likely; though
if I'm still awake,
which is bloody likely,
I guess I'll watch
it. I remember how
lovely Julianna
Slosson looked coming
down the aisle. All
in white and lace!
But that was plenty
some years ago. And
it sure is hot, muggy
July.

At Darragh's I

lie in bed and watch the night
rise slowly, implacably, out of
evening, darkening
the lance-shaped leaves of that
nut tree whose name I never
can remember: only, those leaves
are too wide to be called
lanceolate: why, they're oval!
(A childhood memory, the
cookies that were called "fruited
ovals," molasses with a
white icing, that came from the
grocer, not made at home, and
oval
oval
oval.) When a firefly dances
into my view (a black window):
another childhood memory:
in Maryland we used to catch
them and put them in jars
and watch their silent, sexy
signal. We also used to tear
their phosphor off: children
can be real fun people!

Or I sit on the porch as
a light rain slants down
onto the pond Darragh made,
the wind riffling the water
and the rain making rain rings
on it. Oriane, the lurcher,
wants in, wants out, full
of the *va et vient* of life
(speaking of French, did
you know that in Paris bi-
sexuality is known as

voile et vapeur? I
like that).

Then we all pile into
the Toyota and drive off
into the
World of Roses.

White

I came back from Cape Cod
last night (Cape Cod? So
for away, so long ago) and
found "they" had, as I
asked them to, painted my
hall and bathroom fresh
stark white! White as snow,
white as an icebox:
too white: I wish I had
asked for a light pink, or
pale blue with white trim
or lemon yellow. Or perhaps
had it papered in some
design or other. Oh well,
there's nothing really
wrong with white. And the
dum-dums shut the French
windows, which I had care-
fully left open, so the
place really stank, reeked
of paint: not nice oil
paint and turpentine, but
latex, rubber-base paint,
like old tires burning. It's
airing out. Only now, by
contrast, the big room,
the room where I live and
read and eat and write and
listen to music and watch
the tube and dish with Helena
and Tom, looks distinctly
shabby: it will have to be
painted too. Perhaps also
white, but with a French blue
ceiling. Now, I think I'll go
and take a dump
in my snowdrop-colored bathroom.

Dear Joe

for Joe Brainard

I can easily believe that I
am fifty-eight, but that you
are forty fills me with wonder! I remember
how young you seemed (and were)
the first time I met you,
when Kenward invited a few
of the younger poets
(Ted, Tony) to meet me and
you came too. You didn't say
much (you said nothing) but
looked at books in that little
house in Cornelia Street, not
aware of what would come to pass
for you there: why, you came
to live there! And you came
to visit me at 49 South Main
in Southampton, wearing worn-
out shoes. I gave you a hand-
me-down pair of—sneakers?
moccasins? I
forget. My room here in the
Chelsea is bright with art
works by you (a "fake Fairfield
Porter" I especially
love), and though I don't
see you often I think about
you a lot:
for your birthday I would like
to send you a bunch of lilies
of the valley, which mean,
in the language of flowers,
"I love you since long."

Amy Lowell Thoughts

What are you, banded one?
H.D.

The sea opened its lips
blue with cold
and coughed up
a cabin cruiser

Covertly, in the mist,
the sun
is fingering some spruce

Draped one,
speak.
Are you a larch?

Just at the surface
toothed rocks
spit foamy mouthwash

The Five Sister birch clump
chopped down.
Thoughts
of Charlotte Mew.

Over the sea
she strolls
in fog shoes

The Morning

breaks in splendor on
the window glass of
the French doors to
the shallow balcony
of my room with a
cast-iron balustrade
in a design of flowers,
mechanical and coarse
and painted black:
sunbursts of a coolish
morning in July. I
almost accept the fact
that I am not in
the country, where I
long to be, but in
this place of glass
and stone—and metal,
let's not forget
metal—where traffic sounds and the day
is well begun. So
be it, morning.

October 5, 1981

"A chance of a few morning sprinkles . . ."
says the weather on the air. It's
October, my favorite month, and where
is "October's bright blue weather"?
Day after day of it, gray after gray:
this isn't the October I know
and love, leaves turning, that
scintillating sky . . .

Moon

Last night there was
a lunar eclipse: the
shadow of the earth
passed over the moon.
I was too laze-a-bed
to get up and go out
and watch it. Besides,
a lunar eclipse doesn't
amount to much unless
it's over water or
over an apple orchard,
or perhaps a field,
a field of wheat or
just a field, the kind
where wildflowers
ramp. Still, I'm sorry
now I didn't go out
to see it (the lunar
eclipse) last night,
when I lay abed instead
and watched *The
Jeffersons*, a very
funny show, I think.
And now the sun shines
down in silent brightness,
on me and my possessions,
which I have named,
New York.

Virginia Woolf

I wish I had been at Rodmell
to parlay with Virginia Woolf
when she was about to take
that fatal walk: "I know you're
sick, but you'll be well
again: trust me: I've been there."
Would I have offered to take
her place, for me to die and
she to live? I think not. Each
has his "fiery particle"
to fan into flame for his own
sake. So, no. But still I
wish I'd been there, before she
filled her pockets with stones
and lay down in the River Ouse.
Angular Virginia Woolf, for whom
words came streaming
like clouded yellows over the downs.

Oriane

My name is Oriane,
the lurcher:
half whippet, half border collie,
bred to course
for hares and rabbits
(there are no hares,
only rabbits):
and so I do,
and chase my rubber ball
and play in waves,
and cuddle
in arms that love me.
This is my home:
its name is
          Oriane

Beaded Balustrade

The balustrade along my balcony
is wrought iron in shapes of
flowers: chrysanthemums, perhaps,
whorly blooms and leaves and
along the top a row of what look
like croquet hoops topped by a
rod, and from the hoops depend
water drops, crystal, quivering.
Why, it must be raining, in Chelsea,
NYC! How I wish I could look out
and see rain-washed grass, and is
it not forsythia time? There, where
I dream of, the elms are gone (Dutch
elm blight), but the giant plane
tree, last to leaf out, last to
shed (but that's not until almost
winter, half a year away, or
so) and the shrub roses, waiting
to do their stuff! Oh well, if
I haven't got that, at least I've
got a beaded balustrade. . . .

People who see bubbles rise

for Darragh Park

may be swimming, not drowning,
or merely diving, rising.
Or watching goldfish in a tank.
Or, "That's a vodka and soda?"
"Yes, please."

I'm on a train (Bridgehampton–New York)
Darragh is with me, reading Proust
—in French, of course: India paper,
a brown leather binding, brown
as the October leaves we pass:
scrub oak, I guess. No, they
still are green. Leathery, but green.

This noon, or early afternoon, I
walked down through still-unharvested potatoes
(one chicory was in blue, blue bloom)
to Sag Pond—Sagaponack Pond, I mean.
Across it winter rye made its
incredible green haze, so soft, so clear,
and trees around a yellow house,
trees I didn't recognize, were
a deep wine red. To their right, maples
did their flamboyant thing.

The dogs, the chat, the dinners,
the insomnia and the sleep:
the lousy book about V. Sackville-West:
for me, a rather mixed-up weekend.
And yet I loved it. I always
love the garden and the house Bob made
and the way the early light comes
in the guest-room windows
through violet curtains. To lie there,
watching it, like someone diving,
who, open-eyed, sees bubbles rise.

Autumn Leaves

Mountains and mountains and mountains
rolling, rolling, rolling:
all overgrown with trees, trees, trees,
turning, turning, turning:
but in the field where we are
strolling, strolling, strolling,
the leaves on trees
are green, green, green.
"Soon," I say, "these leaves,
the ginkgo, the willow and the beech,
will all be
turning, turning, turning.
That smouldering red off there
is swamp maple."

Then we come to a fence
where one who has given
his life to poetry leans.
Next to him a sign proclaims,
ETERNAL HAPPINESS. Am I
dreaming about Frank again?
Frank among the leaves
all turning, turning, turning.

En Route to Southampton

In a corner of a parlor-car
window, a thin crescent is
the moon. Below,
the sky on the horizon
is oily bilge.
The leafless trees go by,
the ugly houses,
the parlor car
is much too hot.
The whistle blows
its warning:
such very ugly houses.
But in that corner
of the window,
the ice-white,
eternal promise
of a new moon.

Tomorrow

for Helena Hughes

is Helena's birthday:
she isn't getting any
younger, but not even
the meanest guy in town
(we all know who *he* is)
could call her old. She
likes to think I'm still
fifty-six, because that
makes her feel that much
younger. Well, I've news
for her: I'm not, not
that I'm all that old!

It must seem a long way
from Bristol, England
(daughter of Irish parents:
the girl with two passports)
trundling, a little
Catholic, in the shadow
of the walls of Clifton
College, where Thoby Stephen,
Virginia Woolf's brother,
went to school, to New York
and the Buddhist Center,
where she does right by
the lamas and . . . and . . .
I love her very much and
wish her all the happy returns she may want, the
bodhisattva of tomorrow.

November

is a nice month to be
born, don't you agree,
Helena dear? We both
were, five days apart:
five days and twenty-
eight years. When I'm
pushing daisies you'll
still be spry as a
chicken. But let's not
dwell on that. A couple
of sexy Scorpios (very
heavy sex sign, you
know), hung with topazes:
golden and glittering,
smoky topazes. November,
the month when the leaves
in the parks finally
come unstuck and tumble
down, bump, bang, the
stately paulownia, the
rugged sycamore: last
to leaf out, last to
fall! Soon, soon. But
no snow: which is all
right with you, though
not with me. A nice
month, though not much
to say about it. So,
as Tom calls you, "the
Divine Miss H.," many
happy returns on your
birthday, many and
many and many. . . .

Fauré's Second Piano Quartet

On a day like this the rain comes
down in fat and random drops among
the ailanthus leaves—"the tree
of Heaven"—the leaves that on moon-
lit nights shimmer black and blade-
shaped at this third-floor window.
And there are bunches of small green
knobs, buds, crowded together. The
rapid music fills in the spaces of
the leaves. And the piano comes in,
like an extra heartbeat, dangerous
and lovely. Slower now, less like
the leaves, more like the rain which
almost isn't rain, more like thawed-
out hail. All this beauty in the
mess of this small apartment on
West Twentieth in Chelsea, New York.
Slowly the notes pour out, slowly,
more slowly still, fat rain falls.

A Belated Birthday Poem

for Robert Dash

You are walking in the grounds
on the second day of summer
taking snapshots, the seeds
of future paintings, under
a June sun already hot
on this Sunday morning.
A red-winged blackbird sits
on the finest top (the
growing point) of a ginkgo
or maidenhair tree.
You got up at seven and went
right to work: how I envy
you your creative energy!
Painting, painting: landscapes
of Sagaponack.
You make houses out of
sheds. You cook, you
garden: how you garden!
One of the best I've ever seen.
"It's a sort of English cottage garden."
"It's a seaside garden," D. V.
flatly stated. Those dummies
what do they know? The big
thrill these past few days
is the opening of the evening primroses
—*Oenothera missourensis,* perhaps?
I love them, their lacquered
yellow petals and a touch
of orangey red. You mowed
the small field (I'd heard)
and I was worried. I like it
when the wind-bent grasses
rush right up to a house.
But you were right: how
the mowed grass (you
almost might call it a lawn)
sets off the giant shrubs

of dog roses, drenched in white
so you hardly see the green
that sets them off. Last evening
the young honey locust gleamed
against a sunset of fire
and green, blue-green. I
can't describe the color
of that tree. Imagine—
no, I can't do it. The roof
of your grand *couloir*
sprang some heavy leaks
in the last cloudburst.
It's going to cost a mint
to fix it: tar and pebbles.
It will cost a mint and
where will the moola
come from? Don't worry,
it always comes, to you
at least (somehow, we get
through). I sit at the dining table
staring out at a dark pink weigela—
it's going over. For your
birthday I gave you five
of the rose Cornelia. They're
pretty shrimpy but will
grow to great shrubs, the canes
bending, studded with
many-petalled blooms: how
I wish I had the dough
to shower you with shrub
roses! But I haven't. I
sit and stare at a blue sky
lightly dashed with morning
clouds and think about
these paintings, this house,
this garden, all as beautiful
as your solitary inner life.
Your moon last night was gibbous.

Poem

I got my hair cut
 and it rains
I'm waiting for the papers
 and it rains
I'm waiting for pretty Helena
 and it rains.

Red Brick and Brown Stone

He arises. Oriane
the lurcher wants
her walk. Out into
the freeze. Oriane
pees and shits. The
shit is scooped up
in a doggy bag, ac-
cording to law ($100
fine) and is disposed
of somewhere.
The sun peers down
and sees them. Ov-
altine, a fag, WNCN:
unspeakable Telemann.
The dinner table is
mahogany and silver
gleams. A carriage
clock chimes eight,
sweetly. The front
room north-facing
studio, its two long
windows divided by
a pier glass. Canvas,
eight by six, cars
charge down Ninth
Avenue straight at
you. Parked, a yellow
cab. A bending tree.
London Terrace, an
eighteenth-century
house now a shop,
work in progress.
Brush in pigment:
scrub stroke scour.
Hours pass. Hunger
strikes: Empire Diner
silver metal art deco.

A porkburger, salad,
tea (iced). Home. Oriane
wants out. So they do
as before. Oriane goes
home. Off by cab to
Florentine palazzo
Racquet Club: naked,
the pool, plunge, how
many laps? Home. (Through-
out the day, numerous
cigarettes. I forget
which brand. Tareytons.)
A pencil drawing of
a vase of parrot tulips.
Records: Richter:
Scriabin: Tosca: "Mario!
Mario! Mario!" "I
lived for art, I
lived for love." Sup-
per: a can of baked
beans, a cup of raspberry
yoghurt. Perrier. Out?
A flick? An A.A.
meeting? Walk Oriane.
Nine p.m. Bed. A
book, V. Woolf's let-
ters. Lights out, sleep
not quite right away.
No Valium. The night
passes in black chiffon.

Tom

They told me, Heraclitus,
they told me you were dead.

A key. The door. Open
shut. "Hi, Jim." "Hi,
Tom." "How didja sleep?"
"I didn't. And you?" "A
log." Blond glory, streaked,
finger-combed, curling
in kiss curls at the nape.
A kiss, like bumping fore-
heads. A god, archaic Greek
Apollo in a blue down
jacket. Fifteen degrees
no snow. Tom hates that;
me too. "French toast?"
"Of course." With apple-
sauce. The *Times*, the
obits, a great blues singer
has been taken from us
and a businessman. OJ,
coffee with milk, lecithin
to control mouth movements,
a side effect of Thorazine.
At the stove Tom sings the
release of his rock song,
"Manhattan Movie." His voice
is rich, true, his diction
perfect. I'm so in love
I want to die and take
my happiness to heaven!
No. To be with Tom, my
assistant, three hours
a day four days a week.
(Tom likes "assistant"
I
prefer "secretary."
No sweat: "Ain't no
flies on the lamb
of God." Ahem. Phlegm.)

Tom's eyes are "twin
compendious blue oceans in
which white sails and
gulls wildly fly." We'll
never make it. Tom's
twenty-eight, I'm fifty-
six: he isn't Proust's
"young man born to love
elderly men." He loves E.
an eighteen-year-old
poet, whose mother feels
concern at Tom's two-
year pursuit (they only
lately made it). I'm
going to tell her how
lucky her son is, if he
is to have a homosexual
episode (or be one, as
I think he is, pretty
boy), to have a lover so
kind, so loving, so
witty—that thrash-about
laugh—I've said it
and I will. At Number
One Fifth Avenue I tell
E., "You should un-
reservedly make love
to Tom and be cosy and
tender." "I'm sorry, I
don't feel that way
about him." Later
he tells Tom,
"We had a man-
to-man talk." Sad.
I only care about Tom's
happiness. "He's not
very sexually oriented.
Here." The French toast
and applesauce are
delicious. We settle down
to read: he, a Ross

Macdonald, me *Phineas
Redux*. How superb is
Mme. Goesler when she
repudiates the Duke of
Omnium's bequest of priceless
pearls and diamonds and
a fortune (she already
has one) so they will
go to Lady Glencora, the
rightful heir, and no one
can ever say her three years'
tenderness to the dying
man was motivated. In
Tom's book a corpse is
found in corrupt upper-
middle-class L.A., where
he comes from. Beauty.
We might some
day shower
together, wash
each other's back.
Travelling share a bed.
Flesh on flesh,
a head pillowed
on an arm. Touch.
Running from a cab to
the deli, the energy
(graceful) of youth.
Thomas Paul Carey of
Sherman Oaks, California,
who writes and sings
his own rock songs, the
son and grandson of two
great movie actors, the
two Harry Careys. Love
is only and always beautiful.

Tom's Attempt to Seduce Big Brother Steve

"I went
 into
 his

    room!!!!!
in
my
u
n
d
e
r
w
e
a
r

and & and
said,
        "Let's
        wrestle!"

Sleep

with its burden of dreams:
a smart boutique, small,
with a funny counter, where?—
the cliffs of Rome, the seas
of Venice? Italy, anyway. Scraps
of colorful vinyl properly
put on compose an intriguing
rain garment. Chic. And
a costly tweed suit! Who
needs a costly tweed suit?
I can't say I need one, but
I sure would like one. Sleep,
with its burden of dreams.
He was much as usual, my
dearest friend, but why
was he wearing a beautiful
Fortuny evening gown? "Perhaps,"
my therapist said, "he was
not only a good father
to you, but a good mother
as well." What an insight!
(An orgy on the lawn: the
neighbors are so shocked
they won't speak to me.)
Then there was the night
I dreamed I was fucking
you. "Jim," you said, "tell
me you love me." "Tom," I
said, "I love you." Then
I woke up and shed
tears: it was only a dream
and you weren't and never
would be there. That's all
over now, though I still and
always will like to dwell
on your thighs. "Tom," your
Dad said, "you've got

good legs." Why, I
believe you're vain
of them! But that's all
right: anything goes in
sleep, sleep,
with its burden of dreams . . .

The Day

Because of a coolness in the air,
because of the henna in your hair,
(it turned it orange, boy)
because of Helena's perky boobs,
because of Tom's insouciant buns
(M. is really gone on them),
I would like to celebrate today.

But how can I, in this stony gulch?
"Questo popoloso deserto che appellano . . ."
New York. How I miss the country,
how I miss that island in Maine!
Never to gather tiny sweet-scented
white violets again! Never to piss
again out the window on the juniper
while I dig the moonstruck bay!
O bay!

A *Table of Green Fields*

On which to shoot pool (that
boring game)
for cows to munch upon
where lambs may gambol
come spring

these thoughts haunt my dreaming
nights, and when I wake I think
of you, blond curls crushed
into your pillow, one hand grasping
your ————

The year goes by, it's spring
again. I wonder why. I
sleep and wake and take
a little stroll to see
those thin trees whose name
I do not know, abloom, again . . .

Tom's Dream

Tom dreamed he was visiting
Lillian Hellman in her kitchen:
"the famed Miss H." was baking
a ham: for him . . . for her . . .
for them. She took the ham
out of the oven and broke off
a bit of bone to test its
doneness. "It's done on that
side," she said, "but not on
this." Then she put the ham back
in the oven, being careful
to put the undone side in first.
That was Tom's dream, the night
he slept over and came
down with that terrible cold
for which I gave him
Alka-Seltzer Plus Cold Remedy.

Perhaps

Perhaps there's time to write a poem.
There is always time to write a poem.
Not literally true . . . what to write about?
How about, the love I bear thee?

Love, how I would love to bare thee!
In your summer clothes I can see
you're quite a stud. Not mine to handle.
Oh well, the hell with that.

There are plenty of things to write
poems about besides unrequited love.
Name one. Food. Poodles. Old age
(fast approaching). Middle youth.

And so forth and so on. I really
love this day, so unexpectedly
springlike in mid July. If only
fall would come! When Helena and I
are going off on our jaunt to Venice,
Florence, Rome, the beauty spots.
Now I think I'll wash my hair. G'bye.

O Sleepless Night

I lie down and spread my legs and arms
out upon my firm mattress on which there is a
                white
percale sheet and two blankets
with which I never never never never cover myself:
"Jimmy likes to sleep cold," Fairfield
told Anne, after he awoke me with a kiss
in my south-facing room with California
wildflower paper, books (more
in adjoining guest room: Lawrence's room: how's Lawrence?
Is he in Lansing? Still teaching French
at the U? I suspect he is.)
As I say, I lie down, spread-eagle, and
the radio plays, classic, not
rock or pop or show tunes or film scores or jazz or blues:
it merely is (you simply must forgive me:
                you you you you you you you
)
a preference. I love all music
except Bach—I do like the sonatas
for unaccompanied cello: how
many are there? Six,
I'm pretty sure. Divine Pierre Fournier!
He draws the bow across the strings (five? six? seven?)
which are not catgut
                &
the sound box resonates: a cello
which is not most beautiful of instruments (did
I say that I always sleep
with the two lamps on? I like light
at night
moonlight
enshrouded in parchment shades).
I wake up
once or twice
a night
and by the light

(starlight, enshrouded in a parchment shade)
of lamplight
check out the time: three a.m.:
"the Dark Night of the Soul"
about which F. Scott Fitzgerald
was mistaken: he
thought it was some sort of sudden unendurable angst
or anguish or plunge into the pit of hell:
no:
it is the moment
when a mystic like St. John of the Cross

                  kneels outdoors
                      and
                 prays: his
very soul
rises in a beam or column or like morning mist
and intermingles
with the divine essence of the Godhead:
love, love, love,
pure and unalloyed, simon-pure, the real thing:
beyond, way far beyond
all human comprehension:
love, pure love, its essence:
gilded clouds, rainbows, no sky, no moon, no sun, no stars,
and yet
light
gentle and bright
light:
Angels, Archangels, Cherubim, Seraphim and Cupidons
choiring together
melodiously
in song that is not plainsong
to the music of plucked harps, wind harps, o-
                carinas and the nose flute
and the oot of instruments: most beautiful of all,
the pianoforte
      played by Sviatislav Richter
         and Marguerite Long (Vuillard).
         Shit, piss and corruption:
did I or did I not
take my Placidyl, which is a sleeping pill

"take two at bedtime"
and the tiny, tiny antidepressant (I
                    have suffered not one second
of depression
dans toute ma vie).
                    A   WHITE   NIGHT
a sleepless night, total insomnia, no sleep
to lie there
open-eyed
and wonder
dreaming and not dreaming
thoughts stream by
slow, slow, slow, slow, slow, slow,
                    flights
of total recall:
all those telephone numbers and addresses including zip code
almost every word Leopardi ever wrote (I
                    have not read
Il Zibaldone, the notebooks,
                    and never will)
"Canto Notturno di un Pastor Errante nell' Asia"
                    "Sous le Pont Mirabeau
                    Coule la Seine . . ."
          "The Moon has set
                    and the Pleiades,
     the night is passing, passing
                    &
               I lie alone"
               a few words
               more
                    which I
                    do
                    not
                    recall
Upon the striking of the hour of one
I know
decisively as the swift descent of the knife blade of a guillotine
                    that I
will not sleep this night: insomnia, a white night, a sleepless
                    night
          piss

Once,
on the Porter's Great Spruce Head Island I
went
without sleep on
Great Spruce Head Island
which is in
Penobscot Bay
—what was I going to say? I forget. Oh yes
I went for two weeks
without sleep: I lay in the dark
with shuttered eyes and rested:
nothing happened: I
felt A.O.K.:
At Ellen's party:
"Really great seeing you again after
all these years"
and
"I'm Jim Schuyler: I'm a poet: and you are . . . ?"
"Did you see Alex—Alex Katz's show?"
I loved it, most of all Ada
in a sable hat
among a few, few, few,
slow-falling
snowflakes, one
of which had
adhered
to her coat. Also,
something immense called "Their Eyes Met"
the color
about as great as color ever gets
last night I
was briefly brushed
by the wind of the wing of death:
waiting for a cab outside the Chelsea
to go up to upper Fifth Avenue
to dine with Barbara Guest—Mrs. Trumbull Higgins—
when, no, not when
a car was
proceeding crosstown at a
normal rate of speed
when

it spun round twice and
shot up on the sidewalk
brushing against my winter overcoat, which is not lined
with sheepskin
and slammed into the brick wall of the hotel
:actually, to be frank and open and sorta truthful
            (You
                    look like a clean-cut kid:
                      have a linea speed:
                          makes
                    you feel real sexy
                          pop, sip, swallow, rush)
Where am I?
In my room at historic Hotel Chelsea:
Dylan Thomas, Thomas Wolfe, Virgil Thomson, me and
                one more whose name
                    escapes me
                        O. Henry, Brendan Behan

What was I saying? Oh yes
        (and the sheep
         half asleep
         upon the greensward
         sheep
         half asleep
         as they creep
                  creepy sheep

        we're three little lambs
            who have lost their way: baaa, baaa, baaa
              a crystal bead
                  and ropes of amber)
Well, folks, dat's about all
        sleepless night
               A White Night
               a sleeping no a sleepless night
               insomnia
Tom Tom Tom, I want my Tom:
Tom Tom Tom, where's my kiss?
Tom Tom Tom, where are you?
                    Tom, Tom, Tom
why do you not lie beside me

———

I mean to say, why
Oh, tell me why
why do you not lie beside me
entwined in one another's arms
my head upon your pliant marble shoulder
you asleep and me awake,
decked beside me
body pressed body to body?
Tom Tom Tom Tom, Thomas Paul Carey
I love you so: forever and forever and forever
                    and a day
through all eternity
and yet beyond that
                    buona notte
(when the inspiration
to write this poem
came to me
en route to see my shrink
I envisioned
twenty or so pages and this is only six: oh well, can't win 'em all)
Tom, Tom, Tom, sleeping beauty, sleep well, Tom, Tom, Tom
                    "Good night, sweet prince,
                    And flights of angels sing thee to thy rest"
                    "Give me the Knife"

Suddenly

it's night and Tom
comes in and says,
"It's pouring buckets
out," his blond hair
diamond-dusted with
raindrop fragments.

THE FIREPROOF FLOORS
OF WITLEY COURT

English Songs and Dances

Witley Court

In northwest Worcestershire
in eighteen-sixty
Samuel Dawkes installed
the fireproof floors of Witley Court

Put to the test in a fire
the firemen could not extinguish
the fireproof floors
failed to distinguish
themselves and are no longer
really to be trusted

Visitor to Witley Court
enter at your peril

Below the Stairs

1

Anaemia, dyspepsia and ulcer
afflict the chambermaid

It's the damnable food you give her
"kitchen" tea
"kitchen" meat
"kitchen" butter

that force her
to indulge in
unhealthy "between meal" snacks

2

Brown and Lilly Bungalows
Boston Garters Simpitrol

The search for health and pleasure
leads to no fairer clime

Laxton House and Hamble Bank
The Grange and Brinkley Grove

How is it you got out so early?

Oh, the missis bought a vacuum
and it do the work in no time

In a Churchyard

Where droop the little ivy shoots
the sun slants down to kiss
the heaps of mellow headstones
brown and gold with tender lichen

Where soil runs deep and loamy
sturdy, unabashed,
singly, in pairs or in great batches
everywhere the sun shall be their lover,
daffodils!
who need slight wooing
to flaunt their winsome charms

Hats

A cherry-colored picture hat
of Tagal straw, its only trimming
a black-and-white windmill bow
at one side, or in front

A shady hat in silver straw
the brim rolled up
and on the crown a clump
of blue wings from an Indian jay

Frock

I love crystal fringe on a dance frock
and the ripple of light as you pass
in a plain little chemisette bodice
drawn down from your shoulder
by long heavy tassels that match
your tunic of pale rose-pink charmeuse

What Ails My Fern?

My peonies have lovely leaves
but rarely flower.
Oh, they have buds
and plenty of them. These
grow to the size of peas
and stay
that way.
Is this
bud blast?

What ails my fern?

I enclose a sample
of a white disease
on a leaf
of honesty
known also
as the money plant

My two blue spruce
look worse and worse

What ails my fern?

Two years ago a tenant
wound tape around my tree.
Sap dripped out of the branches
on babies in buggies below. So
I unwound the tape.

Can nothing be done
to revive my tree?

What ails my fern?

I hate my disordered
backyard fence
where lilac, weigela
and mock orange grow.
Please advise
how to get rid of it.

Weeping willow roots
reaching out
seeking water
fill my cesspool and well.
What do you suggest?

What ails my fern?

Wild Eggs

For her size the moor hen
lays a large egg
and many of them
and the eggs make delicate eating

By abstraction she
can be made to lay
more than her normal number
and her eggs make delicate eating

Boer War Bread Strike

Oversifted fine white flour
with little crust
and that not crisp

We cannot fight on this glue
give us the bread we are used to

Of stone-ground flour
the kissing-crust
the color of the rest
and baked right through

Bread for bread, bread
for the prisoners
each craving what
from his youth he ate
not the bread of exile
and that not crisp

Procession

Serene and purple twilight of the South
the wind-distorted olives
so dim beside the road
so very still tonight
the sea delicately touches
the shore with foam

Black clad, glimmer of white
pyramids of trembling gold
up the white road wind
in misty iris blue

a cross, a crown, a spear

the air is drenched

the nails, the hammer

fragrance of lemon and orange

the scourge, a sponge

salt perfume of the sea

Adverts

1

Ambrosia

Fry's Cocoa! The word
means food of the gods

So perfect, so peerless
nothing to throw away
more and more relied on

Fry's Cocoa! I repeat
there is no better food

2

Good-bye, Cheap Lamps

What fine lamps
these Mazdas are!

We were wise to say,
Good-bye, cheap lamps

And to heavy bills
for current, too!

Yes. There's no doubt
about it. So-called

cheap lamps cost
most in the long run

In future we
will stick to
Mazda lamps
          with the wonderful no-sag filament

That's what I
call a good light

3

Swan and Edgar   Good Linen

We sleep on linen
we dress in linen
we clothe our table
with a linen cloth

Constant service
lasting pleasure
indeed it is
a royal fabric

Swan and Edgar
          Good linen
Swan and Edgar
          Good linen

A Few Days

are all we have. So count them as they pass. They pass
    too quickly
out of breath: don't dwell on the grave, which yawns for
    one and all.
Will you be buried in the yard? Sorry, it's against
    the law. You can only
lie in an authorized plot but you won't be there to
    know it so why worry
about it? Here I am at my brother's house in western
    New York: I came
here yesterday on the Empire State Express, eight hours
    of boredom on the train.
A pretty blond child sat next to me for a while. She
    had a winning smile,
but I couldn't talk to her, beyond "What happened to
    your shoes?" "I put them under the seat." And
so she had. She pressed the button that released the
    seat back and sank
back like an old woman. Outside, the purple loosestrife
    bloomed in swathes
that turned the railway ditch and fields into a
    sunset-reflecting lake.
And there was goldenrod and tattered Queen Anne's lace
    and the noble Hudson
on which just one sailboat sailed, billowing, on a
    weekday afternoon.
A tug towed some scows. Sandy red earth and cows,
    the calves like
big dogs. With Fresca and ham and cheese on a roll the
    eight hours somehow passed.
My sister-in-law met me at the Buffalo Central Station
    and drove me out to their house.
Hilde is just back from a visit home to Augsburg,
    where she was born
not too long ago. She taught herself to speak English, which
    she does extremely well.

My mother now lives with them in the house my brother built
　　himself. She's old: almost eighty-nine
and her sight is failing. She has little to do but sit and
　　listen to the TV rumble.
When I came in she said, "I can't see you but I know your
　　voice."
"Some corner of a garden where the soul sinks down under
　　its own weight . . ."
But this isn't about my family, although I wish it were. My
　　niece Peggy is at
camp in the Adirondacks so I am staying in her room.
　　It's essence of teenage
girl: soft lilac walls, colored photographs of rock stars,
　　nosegays of artificial flowers,
signs on the door: THIS ROOM IS A DISASTER AREA, and
　　GARBAGEDUMP.
"Some ashcan at the world's end . . ." But this is not
　　my family's story, nor
is it Molly's: the coon hound pleading silently for table
　　scraps. The temperature
last night dipped into the forties: a record for August
　　14th. There is a German
down pouff on the bed and I was glad to wriggle under
　　it and sleep the sleep
of the just. Today is a perfection of blue: the leaves
　　go lisp in the breeze.
I wish I were a better traveler; I love new places, the
　　arrival in a station
after the ennui of a trip. On the train across the aisle
　　from me there was a young couple.
He read while she stroked the flank of his chest in a
　　circular motion, motherly,
covetous. They kissed. What is lovelier than young love?
　　Will it only lead
to barren years of a sour marriage? They were perfect
　　together. I wish
them well. This coffee is cold. The eighteen-cup pot
　　like most inventions
doesn't work so well. A few days: how to celebrate them?
　　It's today I want

to memorialize but how can I? What is there to it?
      Cold coffee and
a ham-salad sandwich? A skinny peach tree holds no
      peaches. Molly howls
at the children who come to the door. What did they
      want? It's the wrong
time of year for Girl Scout cookies.
My mother can't find her hair net. She nurses a cup of
      coffee substitute, since
her religion (Christian Science) forbids the use
      of stimulants. On this
desk, a vase of dried blue flowers, a vase of artificial
      roses, a bottle with
a dog for stopper, a lamp, two plush lions that hug
      affectionately, a bright
red travel clock, a Remington Rand, my Olivetti, the
      ashtray and the coffee cup.
Moonlight Serenade:
            Moon, shine in my yard,
            let the grass blades
            cast shadows on themselves.
            Harbinger of dreams,
            let me sleep in your
            eternal glow.
That was last night. Today, the color of a buttercup,
      winds on the spool
of time, an opaque snapshot. Today is better than yesterday,
      which was too cold for
August. Still, it had its majesty of tumultuous cloud wrack.
      Here and there a sunbeam
struggled through. Like the picture in my grandmother's Bible
      of Judgment Day:
Rembrandtesque beams of spotlights through cloud cities on a
      desolate landscape. I
used to feel frightened when I saw that effect in the sky. The
      August coolness:
a winter's-coming autumn feeling of it's time to pull our
      horns in and snuggle
down for winter. The radio, the anodyne of the lonely, speaks
      or rather sings:

I love you only
don't want to be lonely
delectable, deleterious trash. Three in the afternoon, when
time stands still.
Is your watch right? Rest after labor doth greatly ease. There is
no place to put
anything. These squandered minutes, hours, days. A few days, spend
them riotously. There
is no occasion for riot. I haven't had a drink in years, begging
a few glasses of
wine. I dream at night about liquor: I was mad at Fairfield because
he invited people
to dinner and all he bought for them to drink was a pint of rum.
I poured some for Anne
in a crumbling eggshell. And what does all that mean? I'm no
good at interpreting
dreams. Hands fumble with clothes, and just at the delirious
moment I wake up:
Is a wet dream too much to ask for? Time for a cigarette. Why are
pleasures bad for you?
But how good the tobacco smoke tastes. Uhm. Blow smoke rings
if you can. Or
blow me: I could do with a little carnal relief. The yard slopes
down to a swampy bit,
then fields rise up where cows are pastured. They do nothing
all day but eat:
filling their faces so they'll have a cud to chew on. I'm not uncowlike
myself: life as a
continuous snack. Another ham-salad sandwich and then good-bye.
Will you say no to a
stack of waffles? I need a new pastime: photography turned out to
be just too expensive. I
miss it though, stalking the motif, closing in on a flower, my
photograph of Katherine Koch
laughing and leaning back in a porch that blazed with sunlight.
You went off to Naropa
in Boulder, Colorado, and I have a postcard to prove it.
I think about your
lesbian love for your roommate. You're a modern miss and I like
you as you are.

Today is tomorrow, it's that dead time again: three in the afternoon
        under scumbled clouds,
livid, that censor the sun and withold the rain: impotent as
        an old man ("an
old man's penis: limp as a rabbit's ear"). It's cool
        for August and I
can't nail the days down. They go by like escalators, each alike,
        each with its own
message of tears and laughter. I could go pick beans only Hilde
        beat me to it.
The drive to the village: a whole generation younger than I
        seem to rule the
roost. Where Sipprell the photographer used to live and work
        is someone else's
now. He was a kind and gentle man. I knew his sons. The one I
        knew best is dead
and gone now, as he is himself. Life sends us struggling forth
        like "the green vine
angering for life" and rewards us with a plate of popovers
        labeled "your death."
Where is mine waiting? What will it be like when there's no
        more tomorrow? I
can't quite escape the feeling of death as a sleep
        from which we awaken
refreshed, in eternity. But when the chips are down I plunk
        them on nothingness;
my faith ran out years ago. It may come back, but I doubt it.
        "Rest in peace"
is all I have to say on the subject. I drink too much strong
        German coffee and
can't sleep at night. Last night I woke up laughing from
        a beautiful sensual
dream: a man who looked like a handsome woman who looked like
        a man. He told
me I should read in the sun to get a better color. But oh, the
        delicate touchings!
Venison stew, rank and gamey. Choke it down. Have a dumpling.
        Once again it's
another day, a gray day, damp as a dog's mouth, this unlikely
        August. In the vegetable

plot the squash are ripening, and tomatoes. Perhaps there are
    nematodes: cucumbers
won't grow here. They start to produce and then the plants die
    back. In the garden
(the flower garden) edelweiss thrives and so do China asters.
    Here, at home, I'm
lonelier than alone in my New York digs. There is no one to talk
    to, nothing to talk
about. "Tell me the story of your life," in great detail. Your first
    memory, the scariest thing
that ever happened: travels and food, the works. "Are you really
    interested?" "Passionately."
When you rest your head like that you suddenly look like an
    old woman, the old
woman you may one day become. Struggle into the shower to wash
    your hair, then crimp
it in rollers. You have a corrugated head. Can't you throw
    caution to the winds
and buy a little of some decent scent? Scent is one of the great
    amenities. Smelling like
a whore's dream. The dream shop and the dram shop. Dram shops
    in Amsterdam, old and cozy
enclosing the small fires of marvelous *ginevra*. It burns
    my throat and my eyes water;
so good to be free in the mid-afternoon, free to be a slightly
    drunk tourist, eyeing
the man-made wonders along the Amstel. Go to Naples to buy
    striped socks off a barrow.
Besides the dram shops there is the Pleasure Chest, with its
    edifying displays: pleasure takes
    many forms: keep it
simple is the best bet. I especially hate the picture of two
    Scotties with pink bows
on their heads. Sentimentality can go further than the door to
    the cellar and the
braid of garlic. Guess I'm ready for lunch: ready as I'll
    ever be, that is.
Lunch was good: now to move my bowels. That was good too:
    "Oh shit," she said,
"I stepped in some doggy pooh." Worse things could happen
    to you. Meeting a

man-eating tiger in the street, for instance. A little
        trembling worthless
thing: a mobile. It balances five angels and I lie in bed
        and throw puffs of
breath at it. It does its shimmering dance. Sunday, "the
        worst day," and we
all sit snowbound in drifts of Sunday paper. No news is
        good news but it
sure makes Jack a dull boy. "I can't get in there: my grades
        aren't good enough."
My nephew Mike came home at two in the morning from his
        hitchhiking trip in the Middle West. He
liked Springfield, Mo., the best. I can't make out why: a
        girl perhaps. He's
sixteen and smokes, which makes my brother see red. I wanted
        to ask him if he ever
smokes pot, but a sudden shyness came over me, the way
        the white sky overcame
this bluest of mornings. A sound of rolling peas:
        traffic goes by.
"Is Fred your uncle?" my mother asked out of the dimness
        of time. "No: he's
my kid brother." "Oh, I see." It's time for Hilde
        to brush and comb
her hair, a glory of white. She sits all day, a monument
        to patience, almost eighty-nine
if she's a day. We talk, but nothing comes of it. Minnesota
        winters when the sleighs
whirled over the snow-covered fences and jokes were
        made about the Scandinavians.
Exhilaration: one night we took the toboggan and went
        to Emery Park, where
there was a long, long slide, on which we sped
        into the night. "I'll
wash your face in the snow!" "Get away from me, you
        punk rock rabbit."
I just sat outside with my mother: my one good deed
        of the day.
That day passed like any other and I took the train from
        Buffalo to New York.

Buffalo, the city God forgot. Not even the Pope is going
    to visit it,
and he should: it's the largest Polish city in the world.
    Now I'm back
in New York on West Twenty-third Street with the buses farting
    past. And the one
dog that barks its head off at two or three in the morning.
    I hate to miss
the country fall. I think with longing of my years in
    Southampton, leaf-turning
trips to cool Vermont. Things should get better as you
    grow older, but that
is not the way. The way is inscrutable and hard to handle.
    Here it is
the Labor Day weekend and all my friends are out of town:
    just me and some
millions of others, to whom I have not yet been introduced.
    A walk in the
streets is not the same as a walk on the beach, by
    preference, a beach
emptied by winter winds. A few days, and friends will
    trickle back to
town. Dinner parties, my favorite form of entertainment.
    Though in these
inflationary times you're lucky to get chicken in
    place of steak.
What I save on meals I spend on taxis. Lately a lot
    of cabs have
signs: NO SMOKING, PLEASE, or NO SMOKING DRIVER ALLERGIC.
    A quiet smoke in
a taxi is my idea of bliss. Yes, everything gets more
    restricted, less free.
Yet I am free, one of the lucky ones who does not
    have to show up
Monday morning at some boring desk. I remember the years
    at NBC, looking
discontentedly out at grimy Sixth Avenue, waiting for
    the time to pass.
It did. Pass, I mean, and I took ship for Europe. A
    pleasant interlude

on the whole, despite my operation. I miss Rino, my
    Roman lover, and
often wonder how he is and what he's up to. Probably
    a grandfather by
now. Good day, Signor Oscari: are you still a grocer
    by trade? Did
your uncle die and leave you his shop in the *periferia*?
    Italy seems so
far away (just a few hours by plane), and, you see,
    since I was there
I fell in love with an island in Maine, now out of
    bounds. I'd like to
find a new place, somewhere where there are friends and
    not too many
houses. This summer has passed like a dream. On the last
    day of August
I feel much better than I felt in June, heaven be praised.
    Who said, "Only
health is beautiful"? There's truth in the old saw. I
    have always been
more interested in truth than in imagination: I
    wonder if that's
true? I have one secret, which I sometimes have an almost
    overwhelming desire
to blurt out; but I won't. Actually, I have told it to
    my shrink, so it's
not an absolute secret anymore. Too bad. Are secrets a
    way of telling lies,
I wonder? Yes, they are. So, let it be. I don't drink
    anymore, still, I
just had four double cocktails: margaritas. At least I
    stopped there. I
like not drinking. Hangovers were too horrible. I MEAN THAT.
    Really mean it.
Tomorrow is another day, but no better than today if
    you only realize it.
Let's love today, the what we have now, this day, not
    today or tomorrow or
yesterday, but this passing moment, that will
    not come again.

Now tomorrow is today, the day before Labor Day,
    1979. I want to
live to see the new century come in: but perhaps it's
    bad luck to
say so. To live to be seventy-six: is that so much
    to ask? My father
died in his forties, but his mother lived to be ninety,
    as my mother seems
likely to. In what rubbishy old folks' home will I
    pass my sunset years?
A house on the edge of a small town, private but
    convenient, is my
wish. I won't say no to Vermont or Maine, not that
    I want to spend
my old age shoveling snow. I spent my youth doing
    that. Our drive
was cut into the side of a hill and no sooner
    was it cleared
than the wind would drift it full again. Monotonous
    days, daydreaming
of any place but there. It rained earlier today: I
    lay on the bed
and watched the beads it formed on the foliage of
    my balcony balustrade
drop of their own weight. I remember the night the
    house in Maine
was struck by lightning. It was attracted to a
    metal flue
and coursed harmlessly down to the wood-burning
    stove that heated
the bath water for my end of the house. I could
    write a book about
the island, but I don't want to. I want to write
more novels. I've made more false starts than anyone
    since Homer was a
pup. Now it's dinner time: time to feed the inner man. I
    wish I could go
on a diet of water for a few days: to reduce the outer
    man to weigh what
he should weigh. A letter from Joe Brainard: he's
    my favorite pen pal.

Joe decides what he's going to do, then he does it.
This summer it's
been sunbathing and reading Dickens and Henry James.
And he sends a poem:
"Ah! the good old days!"
"If gobbled then—digested now.
(Clarified by time—romanticised by mind.)
For today's repast remembered."
and:
"Reminds me of you—Jimmy—out in
Southampton in the big Porter House in your
little room of many books it takes game-
board strategy to relocate now, as then."
and:
"Out trekking up South Main Street
you are:
a pair of thick white legs
sporting Bermuda shorts
(of a *most* unusual length)
and plain blue sneakers so 'you'
they are."
I tripped and fell the other night and struck the curb
with my head,
face forward. I went to the emergency at St. Vincent's.
They put stitches
in my chin: I look like "The Masque of the Red Death."
Feel like it, too.
I wish this humid unsunny day would get its act together
and take it on the road.
It's no day for writing poems. Or for writing, period.
So I didn't.
Write, that is. The bruises on my face have gone, just
a thin scab on
the chin where they put the stitches. I'm back on Antabuse:
what a drag. I
really love drinking, but once I'm sailing I can't seem
to stop. So, pills
are once again the answer. It must have been horrible
to live before
the days of modern medicine—all those great artists going
off their chump

from syphilis or coughing their lungs out with TB. But
    they still haven't
found a live-forever pill. But soon. Across the street
    sunlight falls like
a shadow on the Palladian office building. This room
    faces north, which
usually I don't like, but the French doors to the
    balcony make it light
enough. I ought to buy a plant, but plants are too much
    like pets: suppose
you want to go away (and I do), someone has to take care
    of it. So I waste my
money on cut flowers. I'm spoiled: I'm used to gathering
    flowers for the house,
not buying them. Thirty-five dollars for a dozen roses,
    Sterling Silver:
not today. Always thinking about what things cost: well,
    I have to, except
when a cab comes in my view: then I flag it down.
    I'd be scared to
figure up how much I spend a year on chauffeur-driven
    comfort. I'd like to spend
    part of this lovely
day in a darkened movie theater: only there's nothing I
    want to see. Fellini's
Orchestra Rehearsal was too much like *Alice in Orchestralia.*
    Perhaps a good
walk is more what's called for. I could tool down to
    Dave's Pot Belly
and have a butterscotch sundae: eating on the pounds I
    walked off. Or
I could go shopping: I need cologne. Taylor's Eau de Portugal
    for choice. In the
country you can take a walk without spending money. In
    the city it isn't
easy. This soft September sun makes the air fizzy like
    soda water: Perrier
in the odd-shaped bottle from France. I dreamed last
    night about autumn
trees: orange, red, yellow, and the oaks dark green. I
    wish there were

---

something besides ginkgos and plane trees to see short
      of Central Park.
"It does wonders for your back . . ." The radio is on:
      perhaps this will
be a lucky day and they'll play something besides the
      New World Symphony
or Telemann. I could call Ruth and chat, only it isn't
      noon so she
isn't up yet. It still isn't noon: it's tomorrow
      morning. The risen
sun almost comes in the north windows: I see it lie
      along the balcony,
cut into shapes by the wrought-iron balustrade, a
      design of crazy
chrysanthemums and willow leaves. This old hotel is
      well built: if
you hold your breath and make a wish you'll meet Virgil
      Thomson in the elevator
or a member of a punk rock band. I still want to go to
      a movie but
there isn't any. A month ago when I wasn't in the
      mood there were lots:
Flying Down to Rio, Million Dollar Legs, Blonde Bombshell
      or do I date myself?
A red, pink and blue slip on my desk tells me that
      I am going to
spend forty dollars to have a jacket relined. A child
      of the thirties,
that seems to me what you spend for a new suit. More
      money! I got that
cologne: sixteen twenty. Think I'll splash some on
      right now. Uhm. Feels good.
      I think I'll take a shower.
No. That would mean taking my clothes off and putting
      them on again. I
haven't got the energy for that. And the waste of hot water!
      And I should wash my hair.
But that would mean putting my shoes on and a tromp around
      the corner to the
drugstore that isn't open yet. Or I could wash it with plain
      cucumber soap and

rinse it with lime juice (I think there is a lime). I
       think I'll leave it matted
and get it cut—oh—tomorrow. For a while I let it get
       really long, I
looked like Buffalo Bill's mother. Ruth says, "Oh, Jimmy,
       you look much better
with short hair." "Graciousness, part of the Japanese
       character." The radio
is still on. "It's time for one of our classical hits:
       you'll recognize this
one." But I don't. Good grief, it's "Greensleeves." I'm
       a real music lover!
I'd rather listen to rock, but if I tune WNCN out I
       can never find it
again. Last night they played the Brahms Second Piano
       Concerto, which sent
me off contentedly to bye-bye land. The sleeping pills
       I scoffed helped too.
It used to be when I checked out a medicine chest there
       would be lots of
amphetamines. No more. Doctors won't prescribe them.
       I heard a rumor
about a diet doctor in Queens who will. Must find out
       his address. But
Queens seems awfully far to give the day a gentle lift.
       I can do it with
coffee, only that much coffee gives me sour stomach. Urp.
       Belch. Guess I'll
make a cup of Taster's Choice. My sister-in-law and
       Donald Droll both use
that brand. Not bad. *The Burning Mystery of Anna in 1951:*
       I prefer the genteel wackiness
of John Ashbery's *As We Know.* A poem written in two
       columns, supposed to
be read simultaneously: John is devoted to the impossible.
       The sunlight still
sits on my balcony, invitingly. I decline the invitation:
       out there, it gives
me vertigo. People who come here say, "Oooh, you have a
       balcony," as though I

spent my days out there surveying Twenty-third Street:
     Chelsea Sewing Center,
Carla Hair Salon. Twenty-third Street hasn't got much
     going for it, unless
you love the YMCA. I once did. I remember Christmas '41.
     I was in the shower
when a hunk walked in. I got a hard-on just like that.
     He dropped his soap
to get a view of it and in no time we were in bed in
     his room. Sure was
a change from West Virginia. When I told Alex Katz I
     went to college in West
Virginia, he said in that way of his, "Nah,
     you're Harvard." Wish I
were, but I'm a lot more panhandle than I am Cambridge,
     Mass. Which reminds
me, I saw in the *Times* that my old friend Professor Billy
     Vinson died of the
heart condition he knew he had. Billy was the Navy officer
     who, when he was
getting fucked by an apelike sailor, lifted his head out of
     the pillow and
said, "I order you back to your ship." His camp name was
     Miss Williemae.
He was a virologist who detected two new viruses, which he
     named for Chester
Kallman and me: Fiordiligi and Dorabella. If anybody called
     me by my camp name
nowadays I'd sock them—I like to think. I remember how
     I felt when Chester
dedicated his book to me and wrote the poem in "camp": "Wearing
     a garden hat her mother
wore . . ." Bitch. Chester's gone now, and so are Wystan, Billy Vinson,
     Brian Howard, Bill Aalto and Brian's
friend, the red-haired boy whose name I can't remember.
     Chester was a martyr
to the dry martini. So, in his way, was Wystan. Brian
     committed suicide:
Why do people do that? For fun? Brian was the most
     bored and boring man

I ever met. He was what the French call *épatant*: he told
    an American officer
that he was a clandestine homosexual. The officer knocked
    him to the barroom floor.
Brian looked up and said, "That proves it." I could tell
    a thousand Brian
stories, the way some people can reel off limericks. For
    a great poet, Wystan
Auden's dirty limericks are singularly uninspired. Sorry
    I can't remember any
to quote you. *The Platonic Blow* gives me hives. Funny porn
    I guess is a gift,
like any other. Who wrote:
    "Lil tried shunts and double-shunts
    And all tricks known to common cunts . . ."?
A tired newspaperman? A gifted coal miner in West
    Virginia? The morning
passes like an elephant in no stampede. The morning passes like
    Salome's veil. Famous last
lines: "I am still alive!" and "Kill that woman!" Fast
    curtain. The morning
passes too slowly. I want it to be seven forty-five in the evening,
    when I'm invited
to dine on delectables chez John Ashbery. I wonder if the
    cuisine will be
Indian? The little minx took a course in it, after all
    those years in France.
Tall Doug and blond Frank will be there: I wonder about
    David Kermani of the
shoe-button eyes? Lately whenever I've gone there he's
    been out on some
important errand: is he avoiding me? I hope not. I like
    him. What a
devil he is for work. I hope his boss, Tibor, values him
    at his true worth.
The sun is off the balcony. The sun is off: a scrim of
    cloud obscures the
sky. Yesterday was such a heaven day: blue, warm, breezy.
    When I cabbed up to Barbara's
I found the park full of joggers: men and women whose
    breasts and buttocks

---

went jounce, jounce. Uhm: a shave and a splash of Eau
     de Portugal,
Taylor's best. I mustn't use it up too fast: think what
     it cost. The only trouble
with it is that it doesn't hang on: I like a cologne that
     makes people say, "You
smell good," like Guerlain's Impériale. Paco
     really hangs on:
people who say "You smell so good" look as though
     they're going to retch.
I threw caution to the winds and threw it out. I
     would like to go
in the bathroom and swizzle on some of Taylor's best,
     but the maid is in
there stinking up the house with household ammonia.
     "Is that girl who
comes and takes care of you your niece?" she asked me.
     No, Eileen Myles is
my assistant: she comes and makes my breakfast and
     lunch, runs errands
to the grocery store, the p.o., the bank, mails letters,
     and always arrives with
that morning's *Times*. I lie in bed and read the obituaries
     and smell the French
toast frying. Served with applesass. I think I'll
     let her take the laundry
out; she needs the exercise. The sun is off the balcony,
     the air is cool
as one of Barbara's kisses, which don't make me feel
     I turn her on.
Her husband won't give her money to pay the cleaning
     woman and they
have a huge co-op. It is all neat and tidy. Barbara is
     very organized
for a literary lady. She loaned me a book about Natalie
     Barney I thought
would be fascinating but the writing is much too coy,
     "Amazon" instead of
dyke or Lesbian. I always think I can read anything
     but some things turn me off:

like trying to read jellied gasoline. I could almost
        put a sweater on
the air from the French doors is so cool. But I think
        I like to live
cold, like George Montgomery and Frank O'Hara wearing
        chinos and sneakers
in the snow at Harvard. It was the thing to do. "I'd like
        to kiss Jimmy," said
a dope who came to the door. Frank made a grand gesture at
        me lying reading on
the couch and said, "Help yourself." So he did. I wonder
        what I was reading?
I should keep a reading diary of all the books and mags
        I read, but what
would be the use? I can't remember what I read. I read
        Graham Greene's *A*
Sort of Life and a week later reread it without remembering
        anything, except his
playing Russian roulette. It's a lovely book, the writing
        is so concrete. I
have a foible for books of family life, like Gwen Raverat's
        Period Piece and
Frances Marshall's *A Pacifist's War*. I went out to post
        some letters (Chemical
Bank, Denver Art Museum, Richard Savitsky, my lawyer) and
        the sun was hot. In
the shadows it was cool but when you stepped into a sun-
        spot you felt the heat.
It's a beautiful day, the gray nimbus devoured itself. No
        clouds at all.
I bought the *Post*. More mothers killing their babies be-
        cause they're mad
at their husbands. What kind of sense does that make? Maybe
        they wanted to have
abortions and their husbands wouldn't let them. How
        does that grab you?
Eileen took the double-breasted blazer Joe Hazan
        gave me to have
the sleeves shortened half an inch. It came from Hunts-
        man! I used to have a

Huntsman hacking raincoat. In Alex Katz's painting
    Incident you can see
me wearing it, flanked by Ada Katz in a hat and Rudi
    Burckhardt with a
camera. That was a long time ago. I wonder if they still
    have their Teddy Wilson
record? The Alicia de Larrocha of the hot piano.
    A few days! I
started this poem in August and here it is September
    nineteenth. September
is almost my favorite month, barring October and May.
    November, my natal
month, is too damn wintry, I don't like it but I like
    my birthstone, the topaz.
In Venice I saw a pair of cufflinks, square topazes
    edged with paste
diamonds—sixty-five bucks, but Arthur, who was
    picking up the check,
wouldn't buy them for me. Cheap is cheap. It was funny
    having no money of
my own. Every time I went out sightseeing I would see
    a black-and-red knitted
tie I wanted passionately to own. Last weekend I spent
    at Barbara's in
Water Mill: a funny turreted house, commodious within
    (this coffee is too strong),
all the woodwork very nineteen-hundred, dark wood balusters
    and cream walls,
Barbara's pictures: Paul Georges, Robert Goodenough, Fairfield
    Porter. We went
to call on Anne Porter, who is selling the house at 49 South
    Main, where I used
to live. The library was void of books: it made me sad, the
    way it did when
my mother sold her house. That one back room in the ell was
    my room. I could
lie in the four-poster on the horsehair mattress and stare
    at Fairfield's color
lithograph of Sixth Avenue and the Waverly Theater en-
    tranced by its magic.

The cover of *Hymn to Life* is Fairfield's version of the
        view from my
south window: the wondrous pear tree in white bloom. Did
        you know that you
can force pears to bloom? Go out in the snow and cut a
        few knobbly twigs
with buds. Soak them overnight in water, put them in a vase
        and hold your breath:
a Chinese print is what you have. A haircut: Breck's
        Shampoo for Normal Hair.
I looked for the *New York Review of Books*, which has a
        review in it of my novel
by Stephen Spender. Couldn't find it. Damn. It's funny,
        having a review come
out a whole year later. Everyone on the street was wearing
        sweaters. There was a
man lying on the sidewalk, one shoe off, his shirt un-
        buttoned down to his
navel. Passersby looked at him coldly; nobody offered
        to help him. I
curbed my Good Samaritan instincts. Poor guy: once he was
        a little boy. How
do you degenerate that way? There aren't any novels about
        blindstiffs these
days: *Tramping on Life* and Jim Tully. Joe Hazan, who lives
        in a Fifth Avenue penthouse,
went on the bum when he was young. I'm thinking about D. D.
        Ryan and her "mothwing" eyebrows.
She says they grew that way, but in a bright light I
        wondered.
She never appears until her face is on. Her boys, Beau and Drew, are
        match-happy. I went
outside and there in the autumn leaves was a circle of flame.
        We managed to stamp
it out. It was right by the house: Kenward's little cottage
        reduced to ashes! Almost.
D. D.'s Vuitton cosmetic trunk that weighed a ton. When we
        stopped at the diner
in Rutland I saw a stark-naked man in the john. He dashed
        into a stall and hid

---

himself. "I really hate to do this," D. D. said, passing a
  car on the right
at ninety miles an hour. *"On ne voit pas le rivage de la
  mort deux fois, D. D.,"*
as Racine said. When we got to New York Kenward and I
  went to Casey's
and got hysterical with laughter.
Blossoming afternoon, what can I tell you? You tell me that
  my hair is clean and cut.
Breck's Shampoo for Normal Hair, 40¢ off. It's nice and
  gloopy. I'd like to
take a bubble bath but I haven't got the stuff. Bath oil
  is risky business:
it coats the tub with slime and taking a shower is a perilous
  stunt. Help! my Eau
de Portugal is half empty. I've been slathering it on. I
  love it. I ought to
get a Caswell-Massey sampler and see what smells best. Patchouli.
  Vetiver (ugh). September
evening, what have you to say to me? Tell me the time. Still
  two and three-quarter hours
until John's. I'm reading Osbert Sitwell's autobiography
  stitched in brocade. I
read a page, then rush back to my poem. I would once have
  thought that Sitwell
was "influencing" me. I'm too me for that. Poor trembling
  Osbert, suffering from
Parkinson's disease. I met him at a party Wystan gave for
  them. John was
dashing tears from his eyes: "What's wrong?" "I just met
  Edith Sitwell." Tender
heart. Edith looked less like her photographs. She was
  creased and had that
famous nose. September day, how shall I color you? In blue
  and white and airy tones.
September evening, you give your benediction. Ruth is
  in love with a priest
(an Episcopalian) who smokes grass. Ruth can convert from
  Judaism and wear a
hat in church. "The Overture to *Zampa* led by Leonard Bernstein
  with the New York

Philharmonic." The radio is such a pleasure. A Hand in
	a Glove: a vase
you couldn't believe. "Price includes round-trip air fare."
	Oh, the radio! I
can't live without it. Yes, I must put a sweater on. Brrr.
	September, how fickle you are,
there is the shadow of a flapping flag. The Plaza Hotel
	was flying a Japanese
flag: who was staying there? I have on a George Schneeman
	T-shirt, a plaid
shirt on a coat hanger. Useless gas. Here is my Blue Cross /
	Blue Shield number: 11223677
H08. I don't know my social security number. It's in two
	names: James Ridenour
and James Schuyler. Ridenour was my stepfather's name,
	and when I went to
Europe in 1947 I found my name had never legally been
	changed. Sometimes someone
comes up to me and says, "Aren't you Jimmy Ridenour?" I
	plotz. It's good to
have your own name. Ask me, I'll tell you. It's pink!
	the light I mean
shining from the west on the office building. The sunset.
	That's the trouble with
a north view: you can't see the sunset. North is kinda dreary.
	Will it be dark
when I set out for John Ashbery's? It spooks me. His
	apartment is so nice:
full of French antiques and oriental rugs and collectibles.
	An angel wing begonia
and wandering Jew, peperomia. He has willowware china
	which reminds me of
the Willow tea room, where I used to eat in eighth grade.
	Salisbury steak. Chop suey.
There were motifs from the willowware painted on the walls.
	It's Wednesday morning, but
later than I got up yesterday: the sun is off the balcony.
	There's a chill in the air,
I put on a Jaeger sweater, sand color. The dinner was
	nice: cold soup, veal

collops with a brown sauce, broccoli, noodles, pineapple
     upside-down cake, whipped cream.
The latter had rum in it and I ate it rather nervously but
     it didn't activate the Antabuse.
Rather nervously describes the way I was all evening: just
     sat and drank Perrier
and smoked. Didn't say a word, even when someone spoke to
     me. I meant to say
to John, "Is there any coffee in the house?" Instead I said,
     "Is there any liquor in
the house?" He looked astounded. I faced it out, didn't tell
     him what I really
meant. I have a sleeping-pill hangover; my head feels like
     Venetian glass. I
only took two pills, not three, which puts me to sleep but
     makes me feel crappy.
The *Times* says there's a vogue for pumps: Eileen and I did
     the galleries and I
watched the women's feet: they were all wearing sandals,
     very chic, especially
a black chick who had on a stylish suit. I thought I could
     beat the starting gun
by taking my pills at seven: seven Sleepeze, two Nembutal,
     the scoffed pills, three
antidepressant pills, a red pill that controls the side
     effects of the antidepressants.
I went to sleep like a babe, and here I am wide awake at
     eleven. Anne Dunn is here.
She can't see me until Saturday lunch. I wanted to have
     dinner with her tonight.
Christ, I feel shitty. I took two more sleeping pills and
     what I feel like. Creamed
shit. I lay in bed for an hour; it was torture. It's the
     witching hour of night.
I feel great. This is the morning; it's wonderful. I can't
     tell you about it.
It's a grand day. I feel cold and I
     mailed letters today:
Denver Art Museum, Chemical Bank (that should bring in
     money), Savitsky, my lawyer: he pays my bills, like

the rent ($550). I went back to bed and slept some after
        all. Eleven hours
        all told. Not bad
but I still have the old sleeping-pill hangover. "He brought
        it on himself."
I know I'm going to regret it but still I do it—take that
        one extra pill at
the wrong time. I could kick myself around the block. It's
        getting light out
not sunlight, just morning gray. It looks the way it feels—
        chill. THE LAW FIRM
OF RICHARD D. SAVITSKY, a card says. I wonder if I trust him?
        There's no reason why
I shouldn't. I wonder how they broke the news to him. "There's
        this guy who keeps
having nervous breakdowns and he can't pay the hospital
        bills—state hospitals being of course out of the
question." Bellevue is proof of that: the scary patients,
        the nothing to do, the
insolent staff (that one nice girl), the egg for breakfast,
        One morning I had a bowl of cream of wheat, the black guy
sitting next to me said, "Hunh, putting sugar on
        grits," so this is
what grits are, people stealing cigarettes out of your pajama
        pocket while you sleep,
patients who will share a cigarette with you, you have to
        be an enforced abstainer
to know you'll never give up smoking, Christ I'm cold,
the up in the air TV you can't see, just a blur, the ennui,
        the doctor: "If there's anymore
smoking on this side smoking privileges will be taken away,"
        that's when you know
you'll never give up smoking. When I was in you could
        only smoke if you had money to buy the cigarettes.
I didn't have any money and had to depend on the charity of
        others. It was surprising
how many there were who were charitable. I swore I'd never
        give up smoking. I
did though. It turned me into a fiend. I took up the costly
        cigar. My first cigarette

---

tasted good. I talk big: I have a pain in my chest and
    worry about lung cancer.
Better make an appointment with the doc. I don't like my
    doctors, except the dentist and my shrink. "Come on
in, Jim." "What are you thinking about?" "Nothing." Not
    true: you're always thinking something.
I'm thinking about this poem. How to make it good, really
    good. I'm proud of my poems.
I wrote a poem about Ruth Kligman in which
    every line began "Ruth"—
talk about maddening. Ruth claimed to like it. When I
    told her it was a
stinker she said, "I didn't think it was one of your best."
    I've got to find that
notebook and tear it up, when I'm dead some creep will
    publish it in a thin
volume called *Uncollected Verse*. It will be a collector's
    item. I hate to think
of the contents of that volume. "Dorabella's Hat," "They
    Two Are Drifting Uptown on a
Bus." Bill Berkson asked me to send him any writings I had
    so I sent him "They Two." He didn't publish it. It's
very funny. The two are Frank and Larry. It's not a poem.
    It's a playlet. I used
to write lots of playlets. "Presenting Jane" is lost.
    It was produced. By
Herbert Machiz. It was horrible thanks to Herbert. When
    I first met Herbert
he said, "A nice-looking boy like you shouldn't have
    dirty fingernails." I blanched. I looked at my
nails: I felt creepy. "I work in a bookstore," I
    extenuated. "Is it
a second-hand bookstore?" he demanded. "No,
    it specializes in
English books." "English dirt." I recounted this to Frank,
    who broke out laughing!
"Jimmy, Herbert is a wit." Herbert dropped dead, on a
    rug? John Latouche
fell down a flight of stairs in a small gray clapboard cottage
    at Apple Hill

among the leaves at Calais (pronounced callous), Vermont.
    Wystan died in his sleep
in a hotel in ring-streeted Vienna not far from his
    country home in verdant
southern Austria: Austria utterly turns me off: the
    goldenesdachtel at Innsbruck
is the worst thing, except for the dragon of Klagenfurt,
    Egg-am-Fackersee. The train
through torrent-torn needle-clad (I mean trees like
    spruce, pines and firs)
mountains and granite-boulders, then you're in Italy
    among the lemon
lamps and *"Permesso,"* which means "Move or I will mow you
    down with this dolly of
bricks." Then there's *"Ti da fastidio?"* which means "If
    I smoke will it give you the fastids?"
Then one day
the telephone:
it's Hilde:
"Mother passed on
in her sleep
last night. No,
you needn't
come, it's not that
kind of a ceremony.
Fred is seeing
to it all right
now. The last
three months were
pretty grim."
And so I won't be
there to see my Maney
enearthed beside
my stepfather:
once when I was
home a while ago
I said I realized
that in his way he
loved me. "He did
not," my mother said.
"Burton hated you."

The old truth-teller!
She was so proud
in her last dim
years (ninety years
are still
a few days) to be
longest-lived of
the Slaters: for-
getting her mother
was the Slater, she
a Connor:
Margaret Daisy Connor Schuyler Ridenour,
rest well,
the weary journey done.

About the Author

JAMES SCHUYLER was born in 1923. His previous collections of poems include *Freely Espousing* (1969), *The Crystal Lithium* (1972), *Hymn to Life* (1974), and *The Morning of the Poem* (1980), which won the 1981 Pulitzer Prize for Poetry. He has also published three novels, one of them written in collaboration with John Ashbery. In 1983 Mr. Schuyler was elected a Fellow of the Academy of American Poets. He lives in New York.